# Missing

by

## C. L. Tompsett

Illustrated by Nigel Dobbyn

First published in 2008 in Great Britain by
Barrington Stoke Ltd
18 Walker St, Edinburgh, EH3 7LP

www.barringtonstoke.co.uk

Title ISBN: 978-1-84299-625-6
Pack ISBN: 978-1-84299-623-2

Printed in Poland by Pozkal

## We ask the author ...

What's the most important thing that you have ever lost?

I bought a ring when my gran died, so that when I wore it, I would think of her.  On the day of her funeral, it went missing.  I never found it but I never forgot Gran.

"Hurry up, Alex," Mum said. "You'll be late for school!"

Alex was looking all over his room for his things.

"I can't find my tie," he said, "or my school shoes."

"Where did you leave them?" Mum asked.

"I left them by the bed," Alex said. "But they're not there now. Rob must have taken them."

"Why would Rob want your tie?" she asked. "He doesn't even go to your school. And he's off sick today anyway."

Alex went to look in Rob's bedroom. He wasn't there. Rob was Alex's kid brother. He was 12. He was off school with a bad cold.

Alex saw his tie on Rob's bed. His school shoes were under the bed.

*Thanks a lot, Rob. I'll kill you when I see you!* Alex said to himself. *I'm late for school now.*

He ran out of the front door, feeling angry.

Mum waited for Rob to come out of the bathroom.

"Did you hide Alex's shoes and tie?" she asked.

"No I did not!" Rob said.

"Don't lie to me," Mum said. "Alex found them in your bedroom. There's something funny going on round here. I'm not getting you that new Playstation if you don't tell me the truth. And as you told me that lie, you can stay in your room all day!"

*Mum got very cross some days*, Rob noted. She'd been like that ever since Dad had left.

"Go back to your room right now!" Mum told Rob.

Rob didn't mind staying in bed.

He was feeling bad anyway with his cold.

And he had his T.V. in his room.

But she was in a bad mood.

"I shall take away your T.V.!" Mum said, "till you say you're sorry."

She took the T.V. out of his room.

Rob sat up in bed.  He was bored.

Why was his mum so unfair?

Alex often came into his room.  He could have left his tie and shoes there.  It was no big deal.

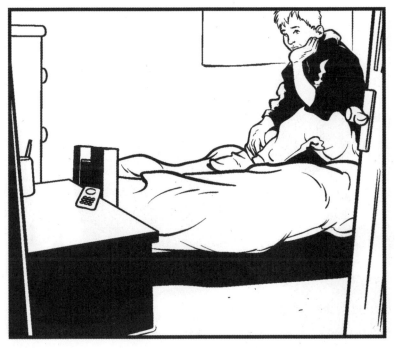

Some time later, Mum came back to his room.

"I'm going shopping," she said. "I'll be back in an hour."

She went to get her bag.

It was not in the kitchen. Or the living room. Nor was it in her bedroom.

*Rob must have taken it*, she said to herself. *He's in a funny mood today.* But how had he done it?

He hadn't left his room. Or had he crept out when she wasn't looking?

She went to his room and asked him, "Did you take my bag?"

"No, I did not!" Rob said.

Mum looked all around his room.

Then she saw it. It was on the table where his T.V. had been.

"There it is!" she said. She was more cross than ever. "You will not get your T.V. back for a week."

Rob's eyes opened wide.

He did not know how the bag had got there.  It was not there five minutes ago.

Why hadn't he seen it when his mum took the T.V. away?

Alex got to school late. His teacher, Mrs Biggs, told him off.

He grinned at the others in his class. One or two of them grinned back.

He tried to tell Mrs Biggs about his missing tie, but she told him to sit down and stop talking.

He went very red.

Some of the kids in his class made fun of him.

After Dad had left, Alex had moved to a new house and gone to a new school.

He felt that no one at this school liked him much. They all had their own mates.

No one hung around with him at break.

No one sat with him at dinnertime.

When school ended Alex went home alone.  He was going to watch his new D.V.D. and forget all about school.

When he got home, he looked for the D.V.D.  He looked on the shelf by the T.V.

It wasn't there.

He looked in the D.V.D. player.  It hadn't been left in there.

*I bet Rob has taken it!* Alex said to himself. *He's dead!*

He banged on Rob's door.

"Have you taken my 'X Men' D.V.D?" he yelled.

Rob didn't move from his bed.

"No, I haven't.  I have not left my room all day," he yelled back.

"That's a lie!" Alex said.  "I hate you!"

Rob got out of bed and flung the door back.

Just then, Mum came out of the bathroom. She was holding the D.V.D. Water was dripping from it.

"Who put this down the loo?" she asked.

"Not me!" Alex and Rob both said.

They would not admit they had done it.
So Mum sent them both to their rooms.

"That's not fair," said Alex, as he
slammed the door. "It's my D.V.D. Why
would I put it down the loo?"

Just then all the lights went out.

Mum gave a scream.

Alex and Rob ran out of their rooms.
They were not afraid.

"What's up?" they asked her.

"I don't know but I'll go and find some
candles," Mum said.

She was fed up.  Was this another trick?

She found some candles in the kitchen.
She lit one.  It went out.  She lit it again.  It
went out again.

"That's very odd," she said. "The candle won't stay alight but there is no wind to blow it out. I'll go next door to see if Mrs Ford has a torch. And I want both of you to come with me. I don't want any more tricks."

Alex and Rob didn't want to follow her.
But Mum made them come.

She'd been funny about being alone
since Dad had left.

"Have you got a torch you could lend
me?" Mum asked Mrs Ford. "My lights have
all gone out. There must have been a
power cut."

Mrs Ford gave her a funny look.

"My lights have not gone out," she said. "There hasn't been a power cut."

"Well, that's very odd," Mum said.

"Has anything else odd been going on in your house?" Mrs Ford wanted to know.

There had been the tie and the shoes and her bag and the D.V.D.  But why tell *Mrs Ford?* Mum said to herself.

"No," she said to Mrs Ford. "No, nothing at all. Why do you ask?"

Mrs Ford looked around as if she was afraid of something. Then she spoke in a whisper.

"The last person who lived in your house left because odd things were going on all the time. He left in a hurry. Aren't you afraid?"

Mum looked at Alex.

Then she looked at Rob.

"There is nothing odd in my house," she said. "Only my two children."

Alex and Rob grinned. If Dad had been there, he would have seen the funny side of it all.